Hello Kitty's
Graduation Day

Hello Kitty's
Graduation Day

illustrated by Jean Hirashima

HARRY N. ABRAMS, INC., PUBLISHERS

Hello Kitty sat on a bench in the park, concentrating very hard.
Graduation Day, the last day of school, was a few days away.

Along came her friend Thomas.
"What are you doing?" he asked.
"I'm writing a speech for graduation," said Hello
Kitty. "I have my notes on all these little pieces of paper."

Suddenly, there was a breeze.

"Oh, no!" cried Hello Kitty as she chased after her notes. "How will I write my speech now?"

"Do you remember what you wanted to say?" asked Thomas.

"Not very much," she said sadly. "I was having trouble anyway, and now I'm really going to have a hard time. What will I do?"

Then she brightened up.
"I have an idea!" she said. "I know
so many smart people. I'll ask each
of them what they think about graduation."

"That's a great idea!" said Thomas.

First, Hello Kitty visited her Grandma and Grandpa White. They were outside working in Grandpa White's garden.

"Grandma and Grandpa White," she said, "I'm trying to write my graduation speech. What do you think is important about graduation?"

"Well," Grandpa White said, "I think the day you graduate is a day when you should be very proud of yourself."

Grandma White added, "You tried very hard and didn't give up. And that's a wonderful accomplishment!"

"Thank you!" said Hello Kitty.

Next, Hello Kitty went home. In the kitchen, she found her mother baking cookies.

"Mama," she said, "I lost my notes for my graduation speech! What should I say? What do you think about graduation?"

Mama handed Hello Kitty a cookie.

"Hmm," said Mama. "I think graduation is a time to think about what a strong and brave person you are. You have met the challenge of finishing your old school, and you know you are prepared to meet the challenge of whatever comes next."

"I like that, Mama!" said Hello Kitty.

Then Hello Kitty found her father who was painting a picture in his studio.

"Papa," she said, "I lost my notes for my graduation speech! What do you think is important about graduation?"

"Well," said Papa, "you and all your friends have developed so many wonderful talents. Graduation is a time to acknowledge all the things each of you has learned to do so well."

"Like painting pictures! Thank you, Papa!" said Hello Kitty.

Hello Kitty found her sister Mimmy reading a book upstairs in her room.

"Mimmy," she said, "I lost my notes for my graduation speech! I'm collecting ideas. What do you think I should say?"

"Well," said Mimmy, "I think it's a time for us to be a little sad, because we're leaving behind some of our good friends and our teachers. But it's also a time to be happy, because we're going on to learn new things next year and to make new friends."

"And we can never have too many friends!" said Hello Kitty.

Later on, back in the park, Hello Kitty talked
with Thomas.

"Thomas," she said to him, "I forgot to ask you
what I should say in my speech!"

Thomas thought about it.

"I think," he said, "that graduation is a great
reason to have a party!"

"What a great idea!" said Hello Kitty.

The next day was Graduation Day, and Hello Kitty had her speech all ready. She talked about how they should all be proud of themselves for working so hard, how wonderful it was to learn about so many new things and to develop new talents, and how happy and sad they all felt on this special day.

"Finally," she said, "we've overcome so many challenges—just the way I did after I lost the notes to my speech—we should celebrate!"

Everybody smiled and clapped.

And then they did have a big graduation party. They congratulated each other, laughed, and even cried a little, too. And before the day was over, they made sure to hug each other hard—especially their sweet friend Hello Kitty.

Illustrations by Jean Hirashima
Designed by Celina Carvalho

Library of Congress Cataloging-in-Publication Data
Hello Kitty's graduation day speech / illustrations by Jean Hirashima.
p. cm.
Summary: Hello Kitty gives the graduation day speech and celebrates with
her classsmates afterwards.
ISBN 0-8109-4818-4
[1. Graduation (School)—Fiction. 2. Cats—Fiction.] I. Title:
Graduation day speech. II. Hirashima, Jean, ill.

PZ7.H3744535 2004
[E]— dc22
2003022143

Printed and bound in China
10 9 8 7 6 5 4 3 2 1

Harry N. Abrams, Inc.
100 Fifth Avenue
New York, NY 10011
www.abramsbooks.com

Abrams is a subsidiary of
LA MARTINIÈRE
G R O U P E

3 8001 00057 6961